Every day he sang, danced, played music and ate to his heart's content.

After a morning of singing and dancing,
the grasshopper started to feel tired.
He lay back on a leaf, dozing in the sun.

ZZZZZ!

The Ant and the Grasshopper

Miles
KeLLY

It was a warm, sunny summer's day. There was a grasshopper in a field, and he was hopping about, chirping and singing very loudly.

Huff!
Puff!

On the ground, just beneath the sleeping grasshopper, an ant was **hard at work.**

The ant's huffing and puffing awoke the grasshopper, who looked down from his comfy resting place to see what the noise was.

"Why are you working so hard? You should be resting and enjoying yourself, like me!" the grasshopper said to the ant.

"I have to work hard. I need to get all of my food stored and my nest ready for winter," the ant replied.

"But winter isn't for months," the grasshopper said. "Come and play with me."

"I don't have time for playing," the ant said. "I have too much to do. You should start collecting food and preparing your home for winter."

"I don't want to WORK, or be inside on a beautiful day like this!" replied the grasshopper.

So the grasshopper kept playing. He sang songs and danced in the field.

Munch! Munch!

He slept in the sun and ate lots of food.

The ant continued to work, storing food and making his nest warm and cosy for winter.

In no time at all, the sun disappeared and the weather turned cold. The field became covered in a layer of frosty white snow.

Winter had arrived!

Brrrr!

Crackle!

The ant was prepared for winter. While the snowflakes fell outside, the fire crackled inside his little nest.

He had enough food to see him through the cold months ahead.

The grasshopper searched for food, but he could not find any. He was very hungry.

And he had no shelter from the falling snow and bitter winds.

The grasshopper remembered
the ant he had met in the
summer. He knocked on his
door and asked him if he
had any spare food.

"Why don't you have any food of your own?" asked the ant. "Did you not store any in the summer? What were you doing?"

"I was so busy dancing and singing and eating that I didn't do any work at all!" said the grasshopper.

The grasshopper looked truly sorry and ashamed. He promised the ant he would work hard next summer and store his own food.

So the ant gave him as much food as he could spare.

It was just enough to see the
grasshopper through the winter, but it
was a miserable few months for him.

Next summer, the grasshopper was as good as his word. He worked hard to store enough food for himself.

The grasshopper
even found time to help
the ant, to make up for
his bad behaviour and
thank him.

So next winter the grasshopper didn't go hungry. He had learned his lesson, and now WORKED as well as played.

There is a time for work and a time for play.